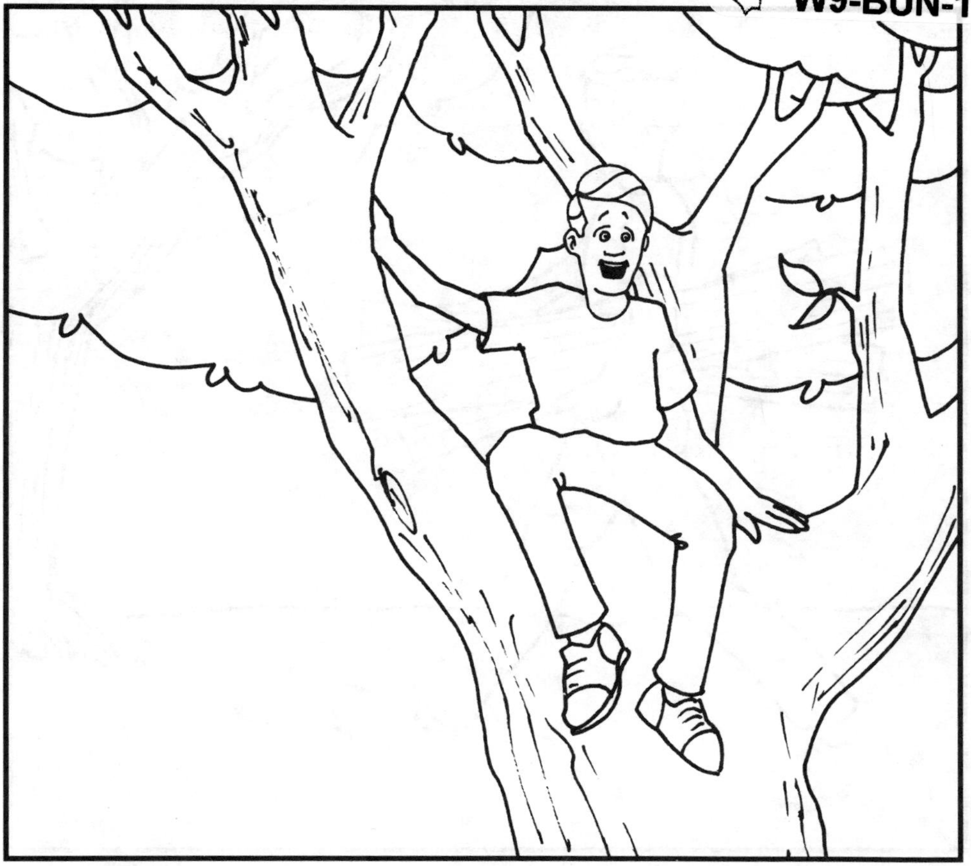

Dad is in a 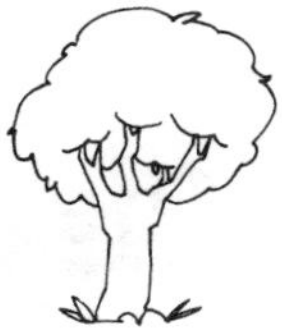 .

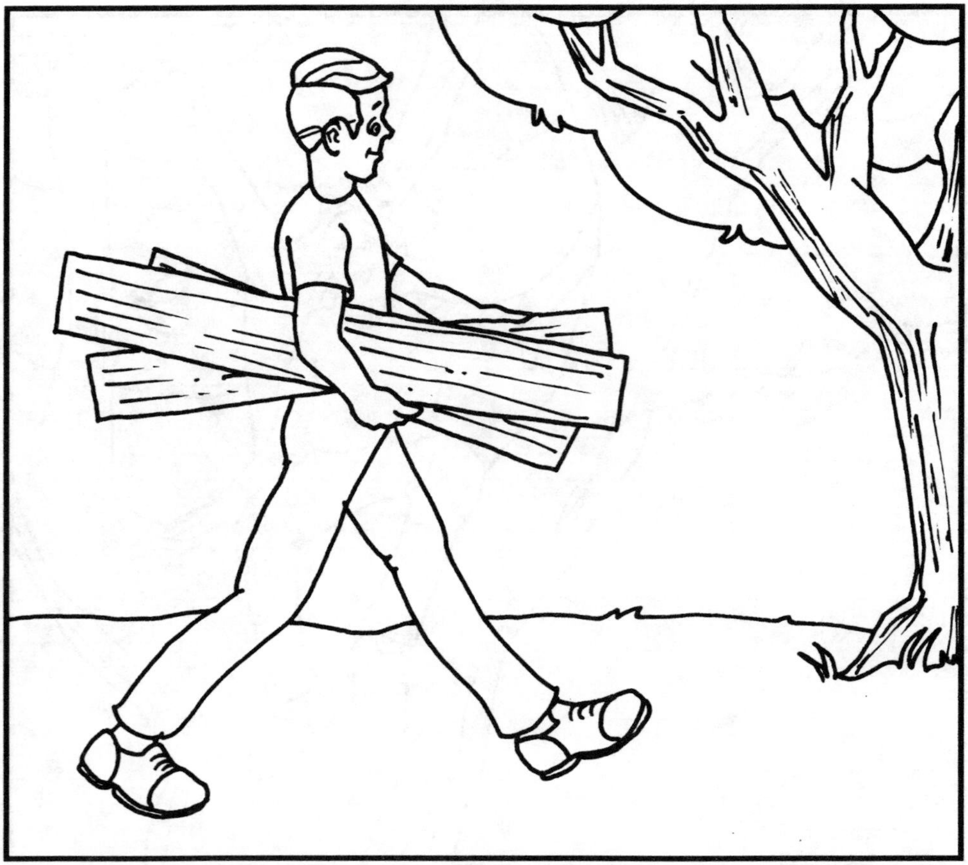

The 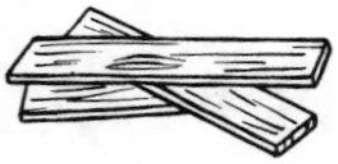 .

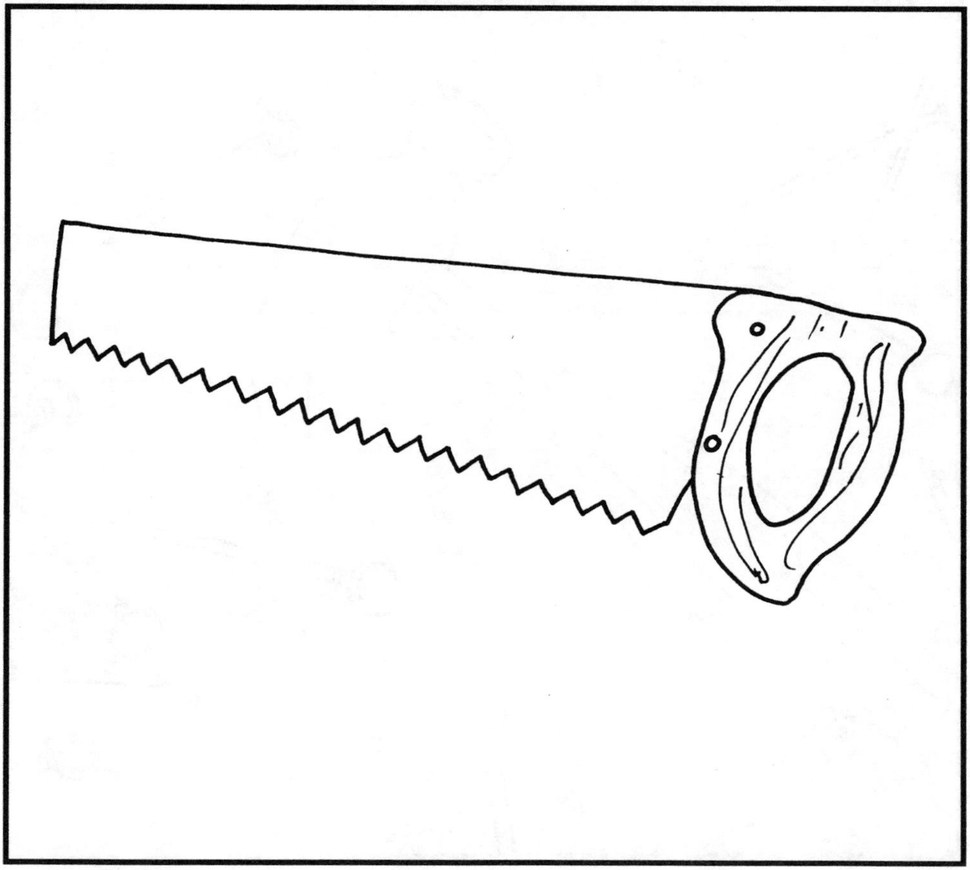

The 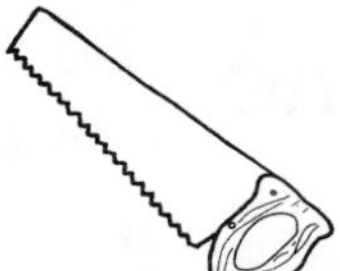 .

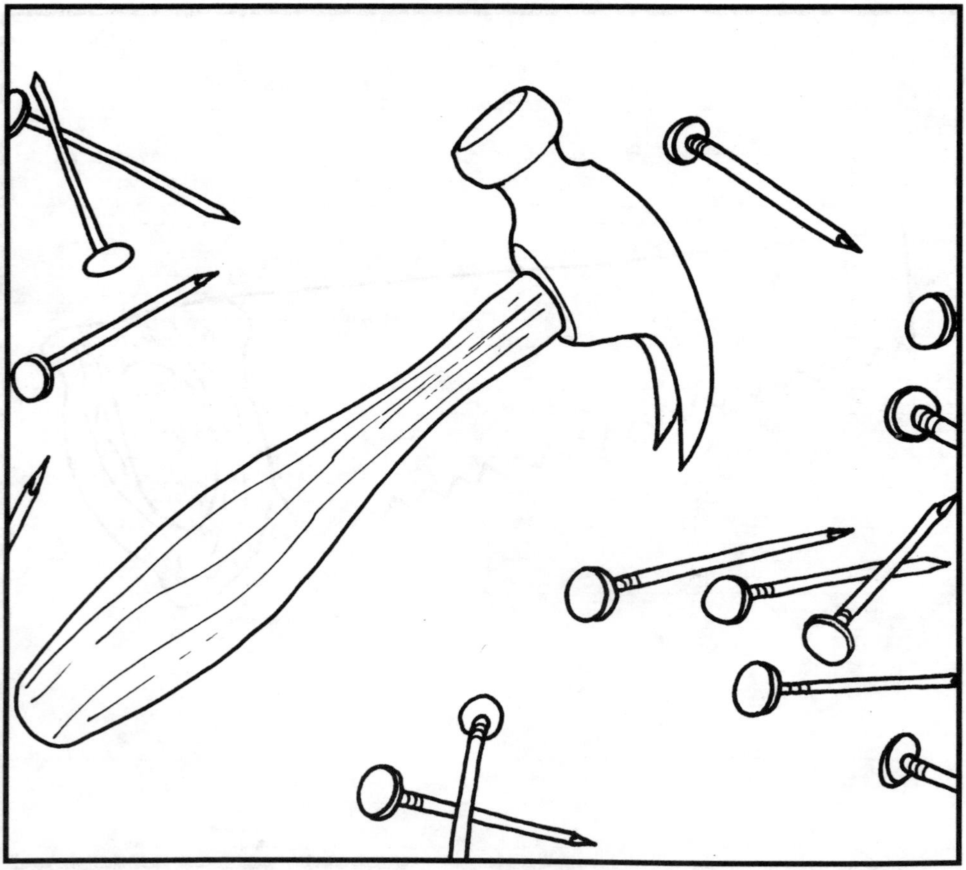

The 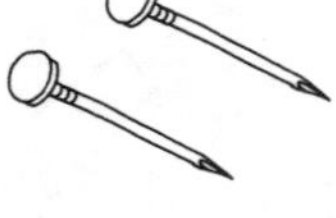 .

The 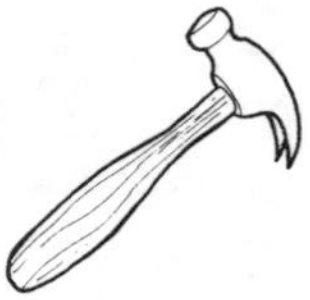 .

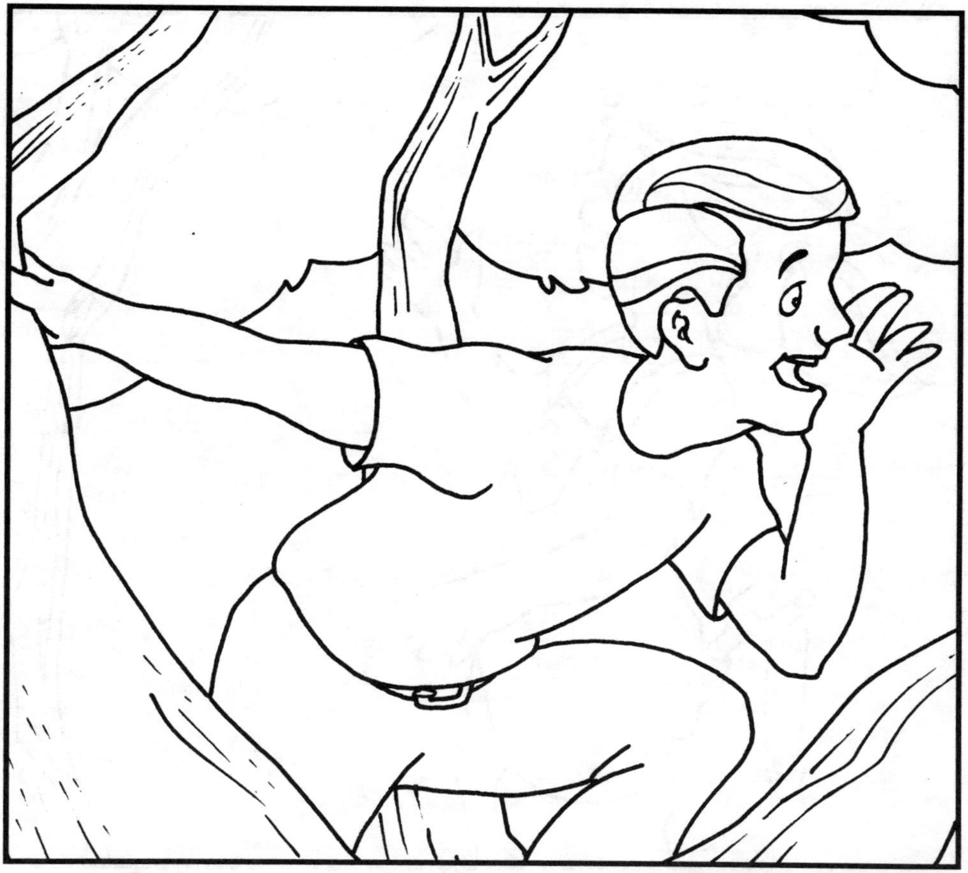

Sam! Sam!

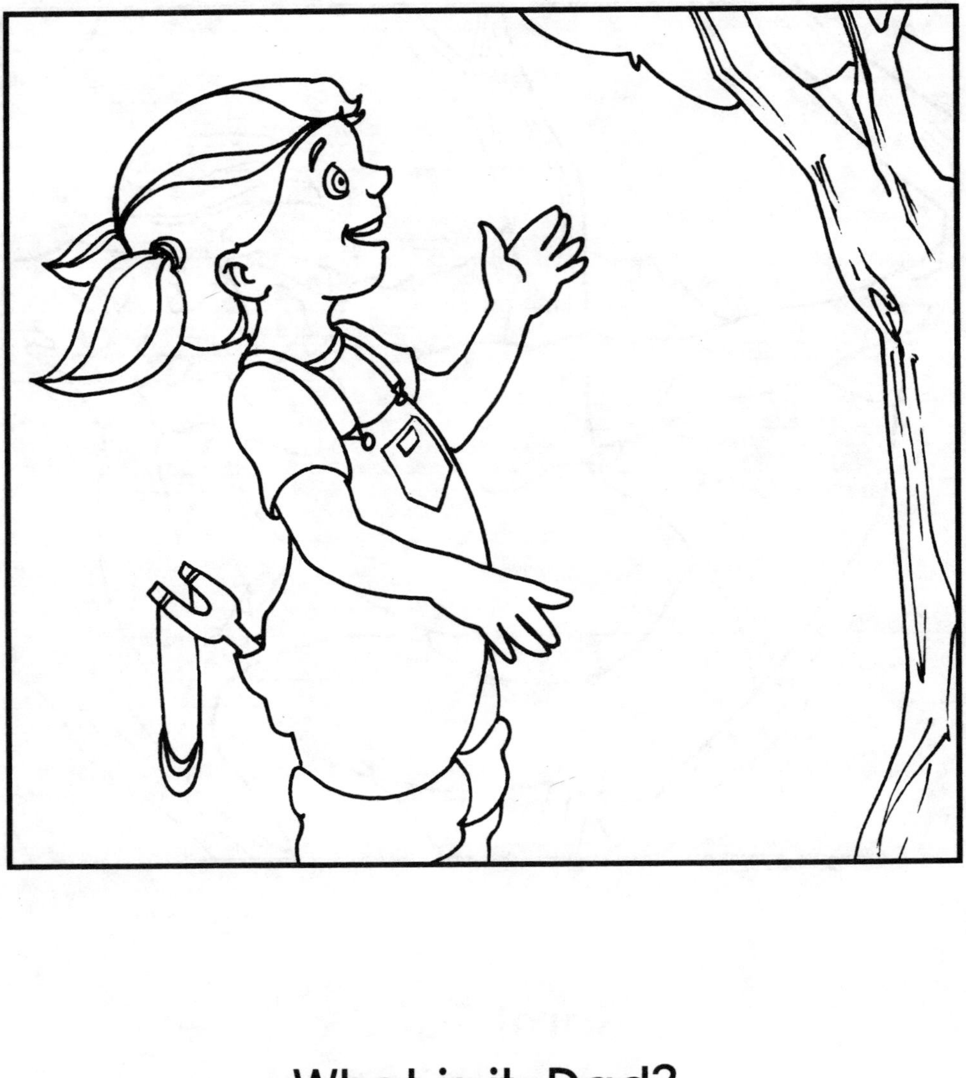

What is it, Dad?

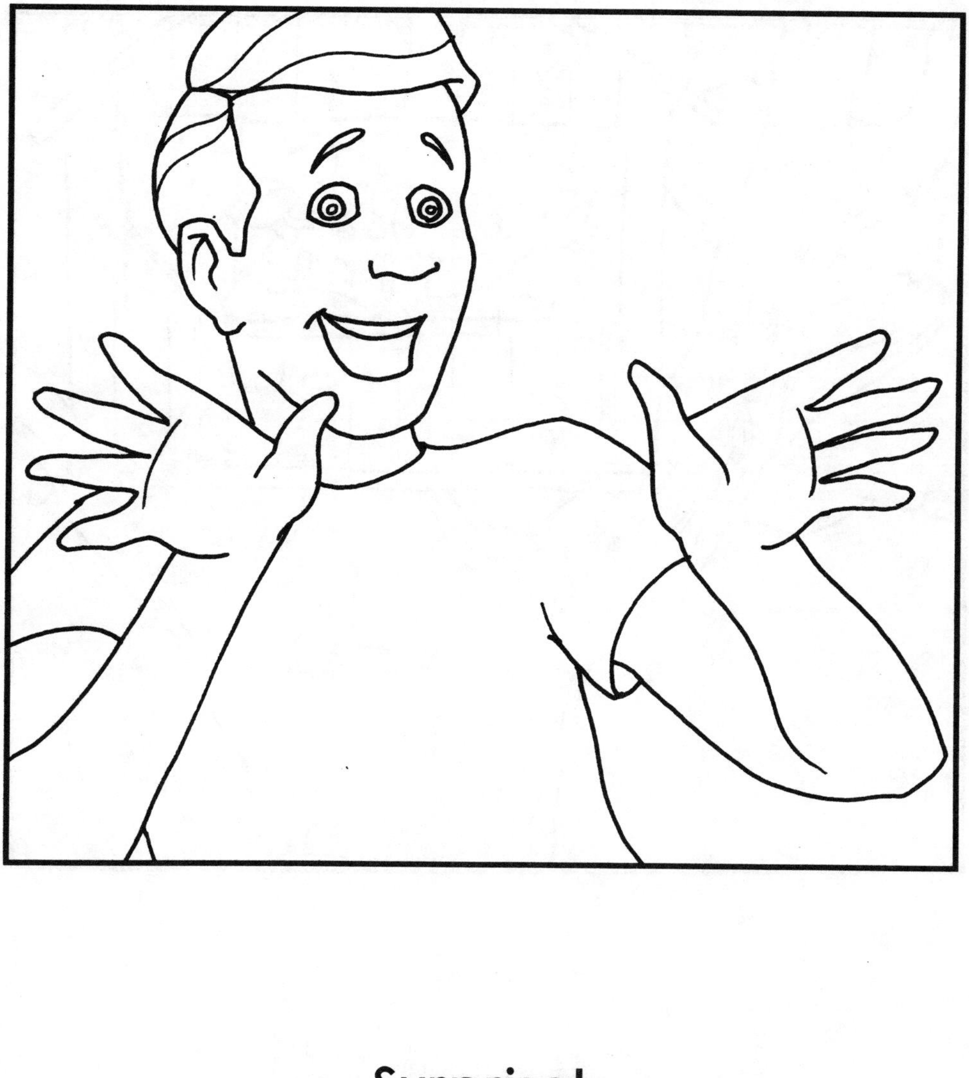

Surprise!

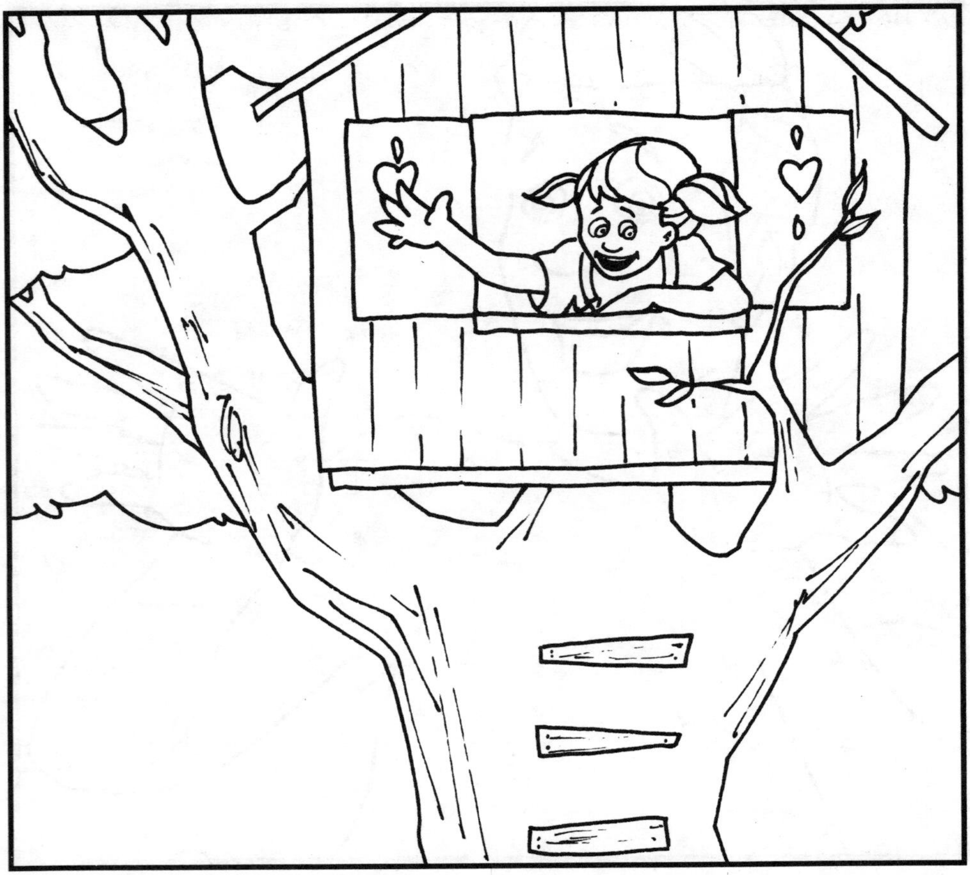

I am in the 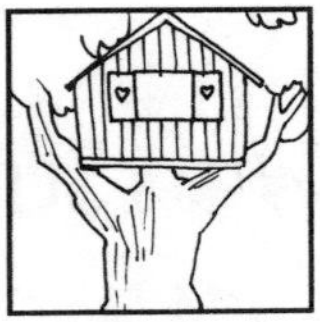 .